B55 022 674 7

Raintree is an imprint of Capstone Global Library Limited, a company
incorporated in England and Wales having its registered office at 264
Banbury Road, Oxford, OX2 7DY – Registered company number: 6695582

www.raintree.co.uk
myorders@raintree.co.uk

Designed by Hilary Wacholz
Printed and bound in China

ISBN 978 1 4747 3951 1
21 20 19 18 17
10 9 8 7 6 5 4 3 2 1

British Library Cataloguing in Publication Data
A full catalogue record for this book is available from the British Library.

All the internet addresses (URLs) given in this book were valid at the
time of going to press. However, due to the dynamic nature of the
internet, some addresses may have changed, or sites may have changed
or ceased to exist since publication. While the author and publisher regret
any inconvenience this may cause readers, no responsibility for any such
changes can be accepted by either the author or the publisher.

CONTENTS

ROBOT
KRYPTO

Behold the secret headquarters of Superman.

The Fortress of Solitude contains a lab, a museum, a zoo of alien creatures and thousands of trophies from the Man of Steel's adventures.

In one corner, Superman safely keeps his mechanical hound, Robot Krypto. Here's the tale behind that artifact . . .

CHAPTER 1

THE LEAD

Superman stands inside his science lab.

He puts down his special laser tools and smiles at his Super-Pet.

Krypto the Super-Dog smells trouble.

"Don't worry, boy," says the Man of Steel. "What do you think of my newest creations?"

Krypto frowns. His tail stops wagging.

Superman approaches a robot.

Krypto has seen robots before.

He knows that they help people all over the world when Superman cannot.

Krypto is confused by what this robot is holding.

In its hands are a bone and . . . a lead!

"Neat, huh?" says Superman. "These robots have helped me many times."

"I figured you should have your own," he adds.

Superman pats the robot's shoulder.

"This is your new handler," says the super hero.

Krypto does not growl, but he is not happy.

He is a Super-Pet, after all.

"I knew you'd like him," says the Man of Steel.

"Go ahead. Take him out for a test drive!"

CHAPTER 2

SMASHING FUN

FWOOOSH!

Krypto flies like a rocket out of the Fortress of Solitude. He leaves Earth far behind.

"I have an idea," says the robot, following along. "Perhaps we can play fetch."

Instead, Krypto heads towards an asteroid belt.

Krypto zigzags between the dangerous, tumbling rocks.

"I get it," says the robot. "We're playing tag."

This game is new to the robot. But Krypto has flown through this asteroid belt before.

He knows every path and every rock.

SMASH!

A smaller asteroid, hidden from sight, crashes into the robot.

Metal and plastic scatter through space.

Krypto soars back towards the Fortress
of Solitude.

He carries parts of the robot back with him.

When Superman sees the wrecked robot, he sighs.

"My new creation!" the hero says.

Superman picks up his laser tools. "The next one will just have to be stronger," he adds.

CHAPTER 3

TOO HOT TO HANDLE

The next morning, Krypto is flying over the South Pacific.

He is not alone.

Superman has repaired the robot handler.

It sticks close to the Dog of Steel.

"More games today, Master Krypto?" asks the robot.

Krypto growls to himself.

Below them, on a small island, the Super-Pet spots a bubbling volcano.

Even at a distance, Krypto feels the lava's heat.

The Super-Pet swoops down and dives into the boiling lava.

The robot plunges behind him without a word.

Seconds later, Krypto flies out and lands on the rim of the crater.

He shakes himself off as if the lava were water.

Krypto is indestructible, just like his
friend Superman.

The robot is not.

Krypto returns to the Fortress of Solitude, with the robot's head in his jaws.

"What happened this time?" asks Superman.

Krypto tilts his head and wags his tail.

"Don't worry, pal," says Superman. "I won't let you down."

* * *

Hours later, Superman calls his Super-Pet back to the lab.

"Meet your new best friend!" he says.

The new robot looks just like Krypto!

CHAPTER 4

LUTHOR

Suddenly, Krypto picks up a strange sound with his super-hearing. So does Robot Krypto!

"Woof!" they bark together.

"Metropolis is under attack," says Superman. "Let's go!"

Krypto barks at the robot.

He and Superman can handle this job alone.

When the two heroes reach Metropolis, they find destruction everywhere.

Superman's greatest foe, Lex Luthor, is stomping through the city streets.

"Prepare for a surprise, Superman!" Luthor roars.

Luthor aims his new weapon.

BOOM! BOOM!

Krypto pushes the missiles away as if they were toys.

"Thanks," says Superman. "But watch out."

"We don't know what else Luthor's new weapon can do."

Krypto barks.

"Give yourself up, Luthor!" demands the Man of Steel.

"Those missiles can't hurt us."

Luthor laughs. "I know they won't," he says. "But this will!"

Luthor pushes a hidden button on his weapon.

Green rays beam out towards the flying heroes. Superman groans, and Krypto cries out in pain.

"My newest creation," says Luthor. "A Kryptonite ray!"

The Man of Steel falls to the ground.

Krypto thuds down nearby.

Both heroes are too weak to move.

CHAPTER 5

JAWS OF STEEL

Luthor stomps closer to his fallen enemies.

He aims his weapon.

"One more blast of Kryptonite," says Luthor, "and that is the end of Superman."

Robot Krypto swoops into sight.

He has been trailing his master, the real
Krypto.

The robot's jaws clamp around the weapon
and snatch it from the villain's hands.

"Where did that miserable mutt come from?" screams Luthor.

"Woof!" barks Krypto.

Luthor spins around.

Superman and his Super-Pet have recovered from the green rays.

High above, the robot Krypto flies at super-speed.

Superman signals to the loyal robot.

"He'll drop that weapon into the volcano and destroy it for good," says the hero.

Krypto barks his approval!

EPILOGUE . . .

Superman clamps a firm grip on Luthor.

"I guess my invention beats your invention," says the hero.

"Ruff! Ruff!" cries Krypto happily.

"You got that right, pal," Superman says.

"Poor Luthor is going to the dogs!"

GLOSSARY

asteroid space rock that travels around the Sun

crater large, bowl-shaped hole around the opening of a volcano

foe another word for an enemy

indestructible something that cannot be destroyed

Kryptonite radioactive rocks from the planet Krypton; different coloured Kryptonite can weaken or affect Superman

solitude quality or state of being alone or far off from society

volcano vent in the Earth's crust from which melted or hot rock and steam come out

DISCUSS

1. Could Superman and Krypto have defeated Lex Luthor without the help of Robot Krypto? Why or why not?

2. Do you think Krypto wrecked his first two handlers on purpose? Explain your answer.

3. Which is better – a robot pet or a real pet? Why?

WRITE

1. Do you have a pet? If so, imagine your pet is a super hero. What powers would it have? Who would it fight against? Write about your Super-Pet!

2. Write your own tale of Superman! What villain will the hero face next? Who will he save? The choice is up to you!

3. Write another chapter to this story. After the story ends, what happens next? Do Krypto and Robot Krypto become friends? You decide!

AUTHOR

Michael Dahl is the author of more than 200 titles for young adults and children, including *The Last Son of Krypton*. He once saw and touched the very first Superman comic book. He is now convinced that he came from another planet and was adopted by his current parents, but they're not giving anything away.

ILLUSTRATORS

Luciano Vecchio was born in 1982 and is based in Buenos Aires, Argentina. He has illustrated many DC Super Heroes books for Capstone, and his recent comic work includes *Beware the Batman*, *Green Lantern: The Animated Series*, *Young Justice*, *Ultimate Spider-Man* and his creator-owned webcomic, *Sereno*.

Tim Levins is best known for his work on the Eisner Award-winning DC Comics series *Batman: Gotham Adventures*. Tim has illustrated other DC titles, such as *Justice League Adventures*, *Batgirl*, *Metal Men* and *Scooby-Doo*, and has also done work for Marvel Comics and Archie Comics. Tim enjoys life in Midland, Ontario, Canada, with his wife, son, dog and two horses.